Caillou®

The Babysitter

Text: Nicole Nadeau, child psychiatrist
Illustrations: Pierre Brignaud • Coloration: Marcel Depratto

chouette

Caillou and Teddy are looking out the living room window. Daddy joins Caillou.

"Look, Daddy. It's raining," says Caillou.

"The trees are very thirsty," says Daddy.

"I'm thirsty too," replies Caillou.

Daddy and Caillou go into the kitchen.
Caillou drinks a big glass of apple juice.
It tastes so good! And it feels good to be
with Daddy.

Daddy tells Caillou, "Tonight Lisa is coming to babysit."

"Why?" asks Caillou.

"Mommy and I are going out for dinner," Daddy replies.

"Why?" repeats Caillou.

Why do Mommy and Daddy want to go out without him?

"Mommy and Daddy feel like being together," Daddy explains.

"Why?" Caillou asks again. Caillou wants to know everything.

Later the rain stops, and the sun sets.
Caillou finishes his supper. The doorbell
rings, and Caillou runs to open the door.
"Lisa!" exclaims Caillou. He is happy to
see her.

Caillou sees his mommy and daddy getting
ready to go out. Caillou had been so
happy to see Lisa that he had forgotten
they were going out, but Caillou cries
when he sees the door close behind
Mommy and Daddy.

Lisa asks Caillou, "Where's that teddy bear of yours?"
"I don't know," mumbles Caillou.
"Let's go look for him," suggests Lisa.

Caillou finds Teddy on the big chair in the living room. "Teddy looks like he's glad to see us," says Lisa. "Why? asks Caillou. "I think he was lonely," replies Lisa.

Caillou and Lisa play with Teddy. Caillou does some somersaults for Lisa.
She claps her hands and exclaims, "Good for you, Caillou!"

Soon it's time for bed. Caillou wants to show Lisa his new pajamas.
"Come on," says Caillou, pulling Lisa by the hand. They leave Teddy behind.

"It looks like Teddy is watching us," says Lisa.

"Tonight, I'm going out with Lisa," announces Caillou.

Caillou and Lisa leave the room and pretend they are going out, just like Mommy and Daddy.

Text: Nicole Nadeau, child psychiatrist
Illustrations: Pierre Brignaud
Art Director: Monique Dupras

We acknowledge the financial support of the Government of Canada (Book Publishing Industry Development Program (BPIDP)) and the Government of Quebec (Tax credit for book publishing (SODEC)) for our publishing activities.

Bibliothèque et Archives nationales du Québec and Library and Archives Canada cataloguing in publication

Nadeau, Nicole, 1956-
Caillou: the babysitter
(Hand In Hand)
Translation of: Caillou: la sortie.
For children aged 2 and up.

ISBN 978-2-89450-706-3

1. Separation anxiety in children - Juvenile literature. 2. Babysitting - Juvenile literature. I. Brignaud, Pierre. II. Title. III. Title: Babysitter. IV. Series: Hand in hand (Montréal, Québec).

BF723.S38N3213 2009   j155.4'1246   C2008-941797-6

Legal deposit: 2009

Printed in China
10 9 8 7 6 5 4 3 2 1